DEMON
IN THE
LAKE

by Anne Schraff

Perfection Learning® Corporation
Logan, Iowa 51546

Cover Design: Mark Hagenberg

Cover Image Credit: Stone (Rights-managed)

For information, contact:
Perfection Learning® Corporation
1000 North Second Avenue, P.O. Box 500,
Logan, Iowa 51546-0500.
Phone: 1-800-831-4190 • Fax: 1-800-543-2745
perfectionlearning.com

26746

Paperback ISBN 0-7891-6662-3
Reinforced Library Binding ISBN 0-7569-4759-6

1 2 3 4 5 6 PP 10 09 08 07 06 05

1 SEVENTEEN-YEAR-OLD Bruce Finley had never wanted to live out here in a place his grandpa called "the sticks." He liked Los Angeles. He liked the action of a big city. But Heron Springs had one good thing—the lake. And on a hot summer day like today, it looked inviting.

"Hey," a skinny, little man with long gray hair said as Bruce started stripping off his T-shirt.

"Hi," Bruce said.

"You're not planning to take a swim, are you?" the man asked.

"Well, yeah," Bruce said. He figured the guy would tell him the lake was polluted. That's all he needed. The one good thing in Heron Springs, and it wasn't any good either!

"Strangers who come to town swim in the lake, but the locals never do," the man said, coming closer. He was a weathered man, about 50. He looked like a gnome.

"How come?" Bruce asked, waiting for the pollution story.

"Something down there in the lake—something bad. It grabs people and pulls them under and drowns them. There's a demon in the lake, boy. You can laugh if you want to, but that's how it is," the man said. He smiled a little and then said, "You must be one of the Finley boys."

"How did you know that?" Bruce asked.

"Not many new folks move into Heron Springs. But we heard about the engineer and his boys coming in to design the big new resort. I figured you must be one of the sons," the man said, holding out his hand. "I'm Oliver McGee."

Bruce shook his hand. "I'm Bruce Finley." But Bruce resented the phrase "one of the sons." For 15 years Ron, Darcy, and Bruce Finley had been a family. Bruce was an only child. Then a good friend of his dad's was killed along with his wife in an auto accident. A 15-year-old boy was left without a family. Bruce's parents eventually adopted Layne Saunders. Bruce had nothing in general against good deeds, but having Layne as an instant brother just messed up everything. The Finleys were upper class, and Layne came from a rough South Central neighborhood in Los Angeles. Layne didn't seem to be a bad guy, but Bruce had not wanted a 15-year-old instant brother at that stage of his life.

"I don't mean to scare you, boy. About the lake, I mean," McGee said.

"Oh, you didn't scare me. I've heard a lot of weird legends about monsters who live in lakes and stuff. Like old Nessie over in Scotland. It's a bunch of nonsense," Bruce said.

McGee stopped smiling. "I didn't say a monster," he said. "I wasn't talking about some big fish or sea creature. I was talking about something evil down there, something that's killing people."

"Well, I'm not afraid," Bruce said. "I'm going for a swim."

"Suit yourself, boy," McGee said. "At least if you get taken by the thing, your parents will have one son left."

"He's not my parents' son," Bruce snapped. Bruce's mom and dad had legally adopted Layne, but Bruce wasn't accepting it. "He's a guy they adopted, that's all. He's not blood."

McGee grinned and something turned sinister in his eyes. "You hate him, don't you, boy?"

It sent chills up Bruce's spine that this ugly, little man could psyche him out so accurately. "I didn't say I hated him," Bruce stammered.

"Bring him down to the lake," McGee chortled. "Maybe that'll solve your problem. Then there'll be just one son again. That's the way you want it, right?"

"I didn't say that," Bruce snapped. "Look, mister, why don't you stop trying to read my mind?"

"Let me tell you, Bruce," McGee said softly, "there was a fella used to come to the lake with his wife when they were kids, not much older than you. Well, seems like he didn't love her anymore, and he got himself another girl, and then she went down in the lake, and everybody blamed the fella. The poor devil nearly went mad with guilt. Everybody was blaming him, saying she jumped in or something. Her name was Rosemary, and the demon got her. It wasn't her fella's fault at all . . . "

"Was she the first one the so-called demon got?" Bruce asked.

"No, there was one before her . . . " McGee said. He sauntered off then.

Bruce went back to the house to get his swim trunks. His family lived in a nice, big house about a quarter mile from the lake.

"Hey, dude, where you been?" Layne shouted as Bruce approached the house.

Bruce hated the way Layne talked. He didn't want to be called "dude." "I've been looking at the lake, and stop calling me 'dude.' I've got a real name, you know?"

"Okay, Brucie," Layne laughed. He seemed to get a kick out of irritating Bruce and out of playing his ear-splitting rap music, which Bruce hated. Bruce liked mellow jazz. Bruce often thought Layne probably disliked him as much as he, Bruce, disliked Layne. They were like two angry scorpions caught in the same bottle.

Bruce slipped into his swim trunks, threw a towel over his shoulder, and yelled back at Layne. "I'm going for a swim at the lake. Some old guy down there told me there's a demon in the lake that pulls people under, but he seemed like a nutcase."

"Good luck, dude," Layne shouted.

There was a little sandy beach at the edge of the lake, and Bruce waded in. He laughed when he remembered what old McGee had said. A nice, little lake like this in a quaint, old-time town like Heron Springs surely wouldn't have a demon hiding under the blue water. Why would a demon settle here? These weren't the dark, cold waters of Scotland.

Soon Bruce was gliding through the water effortlessly, enjoying himself. He had been on the swim team back at his high school in Los Angeles. But now he'd be attending Heron Valley District High, and they probably didn't have a swimming program. Bruce wondered if he'd have any opportunity to play sports.

"I know it's a big sacrifice for you guys," their dad had said to Bruce and Layne, "but this is a once-in-a-lifetime chance for me to design a really great resort. Can you believe they're going to let me make a bird sanctuary alongside the resort? This is no rip-up-the-land type of project."

"Sounds great, Dad," Layne chimed right in. It seemed sometimes that he got along better with their dad than Bruce did. And that riled Bruce even more.

Bruce's dad had looked at Bruce then. "I know you'll be giving up your friends, and I'm sorry about that, but it's just for a year," he said.

Bruce had not answered. Just a year? But it was Bruce's senior year in high school. How do you get that back? How could his dad be so big-hearted and compassionate that he'd adopt a friend's orphan son, but not realize that his senior year means more to a 17-year-old than anything?

Bruce moved through the water like a fish. In the last few months as they pulled up stakes and moved here, Bruce was so angry half the time that he wanted to punch a hole in his bedroom wall. Now, as he swam deeper to the center of the lake, Bruce remembered how Layne encouraged their dad to take the job.

What did he care? He wasn't leaving old friends behind. He'd been in a foster home since his parents died, and he had already lost what friends he had. He had nothing to lose by moving to Heron Springs. It was easy for him to support their dad's plans.

Bruce ducked beneath the water for a moment, and then he sucked in his breath in horror.

He saw a human face down there! During the first seconds of terror and shock, Bruce just wanted to get away from the spot as quickly as possible. But when he made it safely to the shore, he began to wonder if it had been just his imagination. He'd been thinking angry thoughts about Layne, and the guy in the water sort of looked like Layne.

Yeah, Bruce told himself as he stood on the sand. That old guy, McGee, was saying I should bring Layne down to the lake to solve my problem, and the rest was Bruce's overactive imagination. He was picturing Layne dead!

No, that's insane, Bruce thought. He didn't want Layne dead. But the face had to be a fantasy. There was nobody in the water. He'd probably just seen a fish swim by, and he'd put a human face on it . . .

Bruce turned and went back into the water. He had to do this. He was shaking, angry at himself for letting his imagination run away like that. He was a big, tall guy. And here he was shaking like a leaf over Oliver McGee's horror tale. Right now McGee was probably off in the woods, watching, laughing his head off. He'd seen Bruce come tearing out of the water as if the devil were after him . . .

Well, I've got news for you, Oliver McGee, Bruce thought grimly, I'm finishing my swim! He plunged deeper and deeper into the water and even glanced down a few times in the place where he had seen the face. He saw nothing more. Finally, dripping and triumphant, he strode from the shallow end of the lake onto the sand. He put on his flip-flops and walked the quarter mile home. As he climbed the small rise to his house, he heard Layne's rap music pounding. Just listening to the sound almost ruined the good mood Bruce was in. As he came through the front door, he yelled, "Why don't you wear headphones when you listen to that trash?"

"Nobody's home," Layne said. "I'm not bothering anybody."

"Well, I'm home, and I don't want to listen to it!" Bruce shouted. "This isn't San Pedro Street!"

Bruce went into his room and slammed the door. For a while it was quiet. Darkness was descending outside, and a glorious moon was rising. From this house you could see a little bit of the lake. When there was moonlight, it turned the water a magical silver.

"Hey," Layne shouted from his bedroom. "The cops are down there by the lake!"

Bruce went to the window of his room. He saw big searchlights sweeping the lake. And then he saw something else. They had fished something from the lake, and now it lay under a yellow tarp.

Bruce sagged against the windowsill, the feeling draining from his arms and legs. They had taken a body from the lake! A body! He remembered the face staring up at him in the dark blue water . . .

2 "I SAW HIM," Bruce gasped, loud enough to bring Layne to the doorway of his bedroom. "I saw the dead guy in the water!"

"What?" Layne cried. "You serious?"

"Yeah, when I was swimming I looked down and saw this face, and I freaked out, but then I thought it had been just my imagination. But I guess it was real! I was swimming right over a dead body!" Bruce groaned.

When Bruce's parents came home, they had heard about the drowning at Heron Lake. "What a tragedy that it happened in the lake—that's the centerpiece of our resort," Bruce's dad said.

"Somebody said it was a young man," his mom said, looking sad.

"I went swimming in the lake this afternoon," Bruce blurted out, "and I saw this face under the water. It had to have been the dead guy, snagged in seaweed or something."

Bruce's dad stared at Bruce. "You saw a dead person in the lake hours ago, and you didn't tell anybody?" he yelled. "What were you thinking?" His dad sounded furious and disappointed. "That is so . . . so inhuman that you wouldn't report the sighting of a dead person. I'm ashamed of you, Bruce!"

Bruce felt the old, deep resentment seething inside him against his dad. He never talked to Layne like that. He would have given Layne a chance to explain. It was beginning to feel like Layne was the real son, and Bruce was the outsider.

"Dad!" Bruce shouted. "Give me a break! I met this weird little guy at the lake, and he told me some wild story about there being a demon in the lake that pulls people down and drowns them. I just laughed it off, but I was thinking about it when I saw the face. For just a second I believed it was somebody, but then I thought it had to be my imagination. If I'd really believed I'd seen a dead guy in the lake, I would have called the sheriff. Boy, Dad, you sure don't cut me much slack!"

Bruce's dad backed down a little. "I'm sorry I came on so strong, but the way you told it at first, I thought you just ignored the body. Well, you'd better go tell the sheriff that you saw the poor guy," he said.

Still smarting from his father's attack, Bruce drove down to the sheriff's office in his mom's car. Bruce was going to buy his own car in a few weeks.

The sheriff took down Bruce's story and his address and phone number. When Bruce left the office, he still wasn't sure the face he had seen belonged to the dead man they pulled from the lake.

As Bruce approached the house, he heard Layne's rap music blaring, amid the sounds of his dad's laughter. His dad loved slow folk tunes. Now, here he was in Layne's room listening to rap! Bruce's pace slowed. He heard his dad's voice.

"That's not half bad, Layne. It's a peppy tune. Makes me want to tap my feet. I thought all rap was about violence and bad words, but this stuff is kind of nice. It's got a positive message."

"Yeah, right," Layne said, basking in his

dad's appreciation of his music. "Some rappers are good guys who want to make the world better."

"Well," Bruce's dad said, "I guess you're never too old to learn. I learned something about music today, Layne."

"You're not old, Dad. Man, I got the youngest dad of anybody I know," Layne said.

Bruce grimaced in the darkness. Layne was a con man. He knew all the right lines. He knew how to butter up their dad. Bruce's dad, who was worried about his receding hairline and his age lines, was now feeling like a younger guy. Well, why not? Layne came from a tough family background. His own father had not been close to him. He was a good man, but he didn't do much fathering. Layne's family was lower middle class, and they lived on a street where the gangs marked every vacant wall or fence. Layne had really stepped up in the world when he joined the Finleys. Why shouldn't he be grateful to Bruce's dad?

But still, it irked Bruce to listen to his father and Layne acting like the best father-son team in the world. Bruce loved his father, and he knew his dad loved him, but they didn't always get along. Bruce did not go out of his way to flatter his dad like Layne did. He didn't think that's what fathers and sons were about. You told each other the truth. You didn't have to sweet-talk them all the time to prove you were a caring person, did you?

"Hi, honey," his mom said when Bruce came in. "What did the sheriff say?"

"Not much. I don't know. I'm still not sure I saw the dead guy. It was all so unreal," Bruce said.

"It sounds so awful," Bruce's mom said, clutching herself in horror, "that he might have been in the water with you!"

"You know," Bruce said, "his eyes were open. I guess that's possible for a dead guy, huh?"

Bruce's mom shuddered again. "Oh, it makes me sick to think about it. I wonder who he is. Some mother's son. That's what I always think of when I hear of a tragedy like that. I don't care who it is. It's some mother's child," she said.

"Mom," Bruce said suddenly, "Layne and

Dad . . . they get along great, don't they?"

"Yes," his mom said smiling. "Isn't that wonderful?" She never suspected the hurt and anger behind the question. She never saw the malice in Bruce's eyes. "Well, you know Layne's father worked for your father for a long time, and it seemed your dad always liked the boy, even then. He was on the Little League baseball team your father coached. Seems like they always had a bond . . . "

"Dad seems to love Layne a lot," Bruce said, his voice trembling. He wasn't sure what he wanted his mom to say that would comfort him. Maybe that his dad loved Bruce just as much or more. Not that Bruce doubted that. Not really. But sometimes it seemed his dad was so close to Layne in a way that he was never close to Bruce.

"Oh, he does love Layne," Bruce's mom said, unaware of the turmoil in Bruce's heart. "That's one of the qualities I cherish in your father. He has so much love to give, and, you know, we always wanted another boy. We always dreamed of having two boys, and now it's come true!"

"Gotta shower," Bruce said, leaving the room abruptly. "I'm still sticky from the sand . . . "

"Okay, honey," his mom crooned, never having a clue about what the conversation was really about.

Bruce showered and sat down at his computer. He played a game on the computer and zapped half a dozen alien invaders with a laser gun. He couldn't help but see Layne's face on all their shoulders. "Take that, alien," he yelled as each green creature evaporated. "That's what you get for coming into our world and trying to take over. Why didn't you stay on Cyclops or wherever you came from?"

Bruce broke into a cold sweat. The savage slur aimed at the green enemies reshaped itself in his mind, "Take that, Layne. That's what you get for coming into my life and trying to take over. Why didn't you stay on San Pedro Street or wherever you came from?"

The police could not immediately identify the body they found. Bruce looked at the photo of the dead man's face, and he wasn't sure it was the same face he saw in the water. The man was young, probably in his early twenties. He was probably one of the transients who regularly camped at the lake. He'd probably just taken a swim on that hot day, and it was his last. His body showed no signs of foul play. It seemed a simple drowning.

Bruce returned to the lake on the day they reported the drowning in the newspaper. He sat on a rock and watched herons frolicking in the marshy grass at the far side of the lake. He didn't feel like swimming today.

"Hi," a girl's voice said.

Bruce turned. He saw a trim-looking girl in yellow shorts and a striped tank top. She had tawny skin as if her parents came from different racial strains—like Bruce. Bruce's dad was Irish and African-American. His mom was Korean and Jamaican. The girl was beautiful, and Bruce thought he was amazingly lucky she had stopped here.

"I'm Jess Grimes," the girl said. "Who're you?"

"Bruce Finley," Bruce said. "My dad is

the guy who's putting the new resort together. We're in town for a year."

"Oh. Your dad must be a very smart man to be doing all that," Jess said. Bruce shrugged. He never thought of his dad as smart. He was just his dad. He was an engineer, but so what? When he tried to hang a picture he usually mashed his finger. He once put oil instead of transmission fluid in his engine. How smart was that? Bruce's mom was always kidding his dad about his goof-ups, and he seemed to take it in good humor. But maybe Jess was right. You had to be smart to design a huge resort. Jess continued, "I heard that the resort is going to include places for migrating birds. That's so great."

As they talked, the subject of the man drowning came up. Jess clasped her upper arms with her hands and shook her head. "I never would swim in Heron Lake," she said with deep feeling.

"Because the guy drowned there?" Bruce asked her.

Jess's dark eyes widened. "You haven't lived here long enough to know, Bruce.

More people have died in that lake than is normal . . . there are all kinds of scary stories that something is down there snatching victims, some dreadful, evil thing."

"You don't believe that, do you?" Bruce asked, surprised that a bright girl like Jess appeared to be buying Oliver McGee's ridiculous horror story.

"Bruce, come over here," Jess said, grabbing his hand and leading him to a large oak tree.

"Okay, what?" Bruce asked, when she pointed to the trunk. At first he saw what appeared to be scar marks in the trunk, like ones made by hurled knives during target practice. But when he looked closer he saw the names carefully carved into the wood of the tree.

The first name was John Doe. The second name was Rosemary. Then came Arthur, then Willy. Then John Doe II, for the man who just died. "That's five people who drowned in the lake, Bruce," Jess said. "I mean, five young people counting the poor guy they just found. Five people in a little lake like this. Sure, it's been over

30 years, but still . . . something is wrong."

"Who carves the names?" Bruce asked.

"I don't know. A few days after the drownings they appear. My father told me that. He remembers when there was just the first John Doe and Rosemary. Nobody ever admitted doing it. Maybe some kind person who doesn't want the dead forgotten," Jess said. Then her eyes darkened. "Or maybe the evil thing comes from the lake and carves the names like it's proud . . . like it's keeping score . . . "

3

"BUT WHY WOULD something be drowning people?" Bruce asked, bewildered.

"I don't know. Some of the old-timers around here say some people don't want development. Whenever there's talk of progress, it seems somebody dies in the lake. Years ago, the lake was much bigger. Before there were so many houses, Dad says there were beautiful wood ducks and teal and snow geese by the hundreds coming to the lake. Now all you see are those heron and a few mallards. Some people say when the resort is finished, the birds will all disappear no matter what your father says . . . "

"But I can't believe somebody would be drowning people over that," Bruce said.

"I don't think that's what's happening. I personally think something evil is down there that kills for its own dark reason . . . it just grabs people and holds them under the water until they drown," Jess said.

"I went swimming in the lake the other day," Bruce said in a suddenly shaky voice. "Nothing tried to pull me under, but I did see a face beneath me, maybe the face of that guy who just drowned . . . "

Jess made a little gasp. "Ohhh, Bruce, you must have been terrified."

"I guess I was at first, but then I couldn't believe that I saw what I saw. I thought I just imagined it. I sort of laughed it off. Well, anyway, school is starting pretty soon, and the weather will get cold so nobody will be wanting to swim in the lake," Bruce said. "Uh, are you a senior?"

"I'll be a junior," Jess said. "Are you a senior?"

"Yeah," Bruce said.

"Oh, great. Then we'll have a lot of classes together. They mix juniors and seniors at Heron High," Jess said, sounding excited.

And then, just as Bruce was feeling on top of the world, Layne appeared. "Well, look who found the cutest chick in the county," Layne bellowed. Bruce hadn't even seen him coming. He was as welcome as a pair of skunks.

Jess giggled appreciatively, obviously enjoying the compliment. "So, who are you?" she asked.

"Layne's the name. Bruce and I are brothers, even if we don't look it. I'm the cute one, and he's the smart one," Layne said. He had a great personality. Bruce had to admit that. Bruce hated him for it, but he had to admit it. Jess giggled again and said to Bruce, "You've got a nice brother."

Bruce wanted to say, he's not my brother. He's some stray my parents picked up and foisted on me without even asking my opinion of the whole deal. But instead Bruce formed a pained smile. Within a few minutes, Jess and Layne were chatting away about basketball, a game Bruce knew very little about and cared less. But, it appeared Jess shared Layne's love for the game, and they were batting basketball stats back and forth like tennis balls.

It was happening all over again. Layne was marginalizing Bruce like he did with their dad. Layne would be a junior at

Heron, and he'd be in most of Jess's classes.

He'll move in and take her from me just like he took my dad, Bruce thought bitterly. I'll be the outsider again. I saw her first. We were doing great, then he moves in and snatches her away . . .

Finally Jess ambled off with some excuse about not wanting to be late for dinner. But Bruce could swear she saved her sweetest "see you later" for Layne.

"That was some snake move, Layne," Bruce said when Jess was out of earshot. "Just butting in on me and a friend like that."

"Hey, dude," Layne said, "I was just being friendly. Is being friendly a crime now? Can I help it if I'm totally irresistible to chicks and all other warm-blooded creatures?"

He's rubbing my face in it, Bruce seethed. He knows he can do anything he wants and I can't stop him . . .

"Hey, dude, you really look mad," Layne said. "You're not mad, are you? I mean, I didn't mean anything by just talking to the chick. That's my nature. I'm a friendly guy."

Bruce glared at the grinning face before him. "Why don't you take a swim in that lake," he said.

"Ooooo, that's cold," Layne said. Then he laughed. "I know you didn't mean it. You're just letting off steam."

But I did mean it, Bruce thought, turning away. He walked back toward the house, smoldering. He felt guilty for hating Layne, but not guilty enough to try to stop. How could he? Layne was taking it all away, brick by brick . . .

As Bruce walked, he recalled Oliver McGee's nasty little suggestion that Bruce convince Layne to go in the lake. *Bring him down to the lake. Maybe that'll solve your problem. Then there'll be just one son again. That's the way you want it, right?*

No, Bruce argued with himself. He didn't want the guy out of the picture. Bruce just wanted Layne to be somebody else. He wanted him to not get along so well with his dad. He wanted him to be a regular kid who screwed up like Bruce did. He didn't want him to be a guy who walks up to a girl, any girl, and in two minutes she's eating out of his hand. But that wasn't Layne. It would never be Layne.

The next day Bruce took a walk through Heron Springs' small downtown area. He ran into Oliver McGee again.

"What did I tell you?" McGee cried.

"What are you talking about?" Bruce snapped, though he knew very well what the little man meant.

"It got another one. Didn't I tell you? The demon down in the lake got another one. Some poor devil trying to cool himself off from the heat, and bang, it gets him, drags him down like a crocodile does. You ever read how those crocs do it? They see something in the water, and they drag it down and hold it there under the water until it drowns. Simple as that," McGee said.

"You saying there's a crocodile down there?" Bruce asked in disgust.

"No, I'm not saying that at all. All I'm saying is the demon is like a crocodile," McGee said.

"Maybe you're the crocodile," Bruce said.

"Now what's that supposed to mean?" McGee demanded.

"Maybe you hide in the water and pull people down, huh?" Bruce said harshly.

McGee threw back his head and laughed. "A little guy like me? A couple of the men who drowned were big bruisers. Willy was a giant of a man. I never could have tackled somebody like him. No way. Besides, why would I do such a thing?" McGee asked.

"Why does anybody do something like that?" Bruce countered.

Bruce moved on to the one and only grocery store in town. An elderly lady stood behind the counter, and she looked like somebody who would be talkative. Bruce wondered if she would know anything about the people who drowned in Heron Lake.

"I guess you've lived around here a long time, huh?" Bruce asked the woman.

The woman chuckled and nodded. "My daddy named the town. I was born here. I guess I was the first child born here. Daisy Lennox. My family's always run this store," she said.

"What do you think about the drownings at Heron Lake? I've heard stories about there being some evil demon down at the bottom of the lake," Bruce said.

Daisy laughed heartily. "Oh, don't you believe it. It's a lot of nonsense. People drown all the time. I had a cousin who drowned in Lake Erie. Folks just drown," she said.

"I guess one of the people who drowned was a woman named Rosemary," Bruce said. "Did you know her?"

"I surely did. I babysat for Rosemary when she was a little baby. Seen her grow up. She was an awfully pretty baby, but she wasn't very attractive as a woman. She got married young to the first boy who asked her. Some skunk who cheated on her," Daisy said scornfully.

"Do you think she went in the lake on purpose, or did she drown accidentally?" Bruce asked.

"I don't know. Poor little thing was all tore up when her marriage went bad. Dirty little rat of a man, leaving his young wife like that. I'd like to have strung him up," Daisy said. "But most likely she just went for a swim and drowned. Maybe got cramps. That'll happen, you know. I'll tell you one thing, though; everybody blamed the husband. Rosemary's parents wanted to do him in."

"Some guy in town told me the husband was all torn up with guilt when she died," Bruce said. "And then he kind of consoled himself that she didn't die because of him. He believes the demon in the lake got her. That's what this guy told me."

"Yes, the husband felt guilty all right. He was ranting and raving when they buried Rosemary. She's the only one of the drowned people buried in a nice grave with a pretty stone and all. Her parents saw to that. He'd be anxious to blame her death on the demon so it would take the heat off him, the skunk," Daisy said.

"Is Rosemary's husband still in Heron Springs?" Bruce asked.

"You'd think he'd have left, wouldn't you, but not him. He never was worth a lick, but he hung around, sponging off hardworking people, begging for little jobs and keeping his rotten self going.

Back then when he two-timed Rosemary, he wore his hair long and flowing. It was brown like a bear's coat. And he strummed a guitar like the young ones did in that time. Wore necklaces, bracelets, and sandals. All that from that silly time," Daisy shook her head. "He thought he was king of the mountain in those days. Now he's nothing but pathetic. The bear's coat is gray now. I guess his beads all rotted away, and he pawned the guitar for groceries long ago . . . "

Bruce felt a numbness creeping up his body. "Does he still wear his hair long?"

"Oh, to be sure. Looks like a witch now. Or a warlock. Is that what male witches are called?" Daisy said.

"It's not Oliver McGee, is it?" Bruce gasped.

"One and the same," Daisy said. "He's the dirty little rat who played with poor Rosemary's heart and sent her to her watery grave crying . . . "

4

BRUCE HURRIED DOWN the
street in search of Oliver McGee.
He found him sauntering out of a
liquor store.

"You never told me you were Rosemary's
husband," he said in an accusing voice.

McGee spun around. "So what makes
you think you had the right to know?" he
snapped.

"You told me this story of how this poor
guy lost his wife and almost went crazy,
and you never said it was you," Bruce
said. "What's that all about?"

"Okay, so I'm the guy, so what?" McGee
said, trying to hide his brown bag, which
obviously contained a whiskey bottle.

"Maybe you shoved all those other
people in the lake just to cover up what
happened to your wife," Bruce said. "To
keep the demon story alive."

"Ahhhh, we've already gone over that.
I'm not strong enough. Look at me. I'm
five-foot-five, and I weigh maybe 115,"

McGee scoffed.

Bruce headed home, still thinking about McGee's crocodile comparison. It was a horrible thought that there was some monster down there, human or animal, dragging down its prey.

At dinner that night, Bruce said, "They should drain Heron Lake and really see what's down there."

"Drain the lake?" Layne repeated, laughing loudly. "That's the dumbest idea I ever heard. Drain the lake! Looking for a big monster fish? Like, dude, they haven't drained Loch Ness in Scotland yet looking for Nessie!"

Their dad was chuckling too. He almost dropped his spoon. Bruce glared at Layne and his father, sharing their humor at Bruce's expense. Bruce's dad even carried the joke forward. "That would be like cutting down all the forests in California to find Yeti or leveling the woods in the East looking for Bigfoot!"

"What about checking out all the black cats so we can see if they turn into witches?" Layne roared.

"All right, that's enough," their mom

said. "You're embarrassing poor Bruce."

Bruce felt like his face was on fire. He jumped up from the table and slammed down his coffee cup, almost shattering it. He went to his room and slammed the door behind him, causing the house to shudder.

That does it, Bruce thought. They're all against me, except for my mom, and even she was grinning at Layne's ridicule until she realized what she was doing.

Back in Los Angeles, Bruce would have friends he could hang with. That would help. But here he didn't have anybody to talk to. He didn't even know anybody except Jess, and she was probably already interested in Layne. But maybe not.

Bruce checked the phone listings on the computer, and he found just one Grimes in Heron Springs. He took a chance and dialed the number. When a woman answered, he asked for Jess.

"Who is calling, please?" the woman asked.

"Bruce Finley," Bruce said. He figured when Jess heard it was him and not Layne, she would remember she was busy.

But then he heard her voice on the other end of the line.

"Hi, Bruce. What's up?" she said.

"Hey, I was just thinking about going over to Heron High tomorrow and checking out the campus. You know, make sure all the cola machines are easily available. Want to come along and help show me the ropes?" Bruce said.

"Yeah, that'd be fun," Jess said.

"Great. I'll pick you up around 10:00," Bruce said, growing more excited by the minute. So Layne had not succeeded in completely turning her off Bruce. He was still in the running.

Then Jess said, "Is Layne coming too?" It spoiled everything. Almost everything.

"Uh, no. Is that okay?" Bruce asked.

"Oh, sure. I just thought he might like to see the campus too. You guys will both be new students. They've made some improvements over the summer, so I'm anxious to see it too," Jess said.

"Yeah, maybe they moved the cola machines," Bruce said. The minute the words left his mouth he thought, lame joke, stupid! Layne would have had something much wittier to say.

Bruce didn't say anything to Layne about the trip to school the following day. He knew Layne would try to horn in on it, and his mom and dad would be shocked that Bruce didn't want him along. So Bruce just told his mother he wanted the car to drive around the countryside.

When Bruce and Jess got to Heron High, Bruce was shocked at how small and poorly equipped it was compared to his school in Los Angeles. The books in the library looked ancient, and the gymnasium was a joke.

"I guess you don't have a football team, huh?" Bruce asked, seeing no playing field.

"No, but we have basketball," Jess said. "And the teachers are so nice and friendly."

As they walked, two boys fell in step behind them.

"You one of the Finley guys?" the taller of the two asked in a gruff voice.

Jess made a face, indicating she did not like these boys.

"Yeah, I'm Bruce Finley," Bruce said.

"Well, look, do us a favor and tell your old man to cancel the resort. Nobody wants it around here. We like the place just like it is. It's great hunting and fishing country, and we don't want any tourists crowding in," the tall one snapped.

"Don't mind Jimmy Carew," Jess said. "He's a hothead."

Bruce faced the boy. "My dad is going to make sure the natural environment is protected when the resort goes in," he said.

"Yeah, right. Bring in a couple thousand tourists, and everything is ruined. Why don't you and your kind just jump in Heron Lake, okay? Because there's something down there that feels the same way we do about development," Jimmy Carew said. With that he and his friend stomped away.

"Jimmy's father is a big hunter," Jess said. "He resents anything getting between him and the ducks he likes to shoot from the sky."

"Maybe guys like him are drowning the people in the lake," Bruce said.

"I don't think so. They're loud-mouthed

bullies, but they're not murderers," Jess said.

"So you're sticking with the theory that some evil critter is down there, huh?" Bruce asked.

"I don't know. All I know is, don't go near the lake."

Bruce and Jess drove around the valley, and Jess pointed out the topmost hill where a mansion with a red-barrel tile roof and bright white stucco stood. "That's where the richest man in Heron Springs lives. His name is Walt Enright, and he made a fortune in real estate when he was just a young guy. His whole family is gone now, and he's sort of a recluse," she said.

"Well, he's got a great view anyway," Bruce said.

They stopped at a turnoff that overlooked the lake. There were a lot of ducks swimming in the lake, and Bruce said, "I wonder why the thing in the lake doesn't snatch some of them." He peered through his binoculars.

"Maybe it likes ducks. Maybe it just hates people. Or maybe it does get some ducks too. How would we know?" Jess said, taking Bruce's binoculars for a look at the lake, which was about a mile down. Then, Jess's face froze in horror. "Bruce! There's a man struggling in the lake! Look!"

Bruce grabbed the binoculars. He saw a middle-aged man in the water, frantically trying to beat something beneath him away. "Oh man, it's the thing trying to get another victim!" Bruce ran to the car for his cell phone. But before he could dial, a police car began speeding up to the lake's edge. There were many houses with a view of the lake, and somebody else must have seen the struggling swimmer.

Bruce and Jess jumped in the car and sped down the hill to the lake. When they arrived, two police officers had swum out to the man, and now they were helping him to shore. Bruce thought those officers had to be pretty brave to plunge into that lake like they did.

"That's Chip Carew," Jess said. "Jimmy's dad!"

Carew was sitting on the grass getting his breath, but he appeared unhurt. Bruce and Jess were close enough to hear him say, "It got ahold of my feet and tried to pull me down. It was the most horrible thing that ever happened to me in my life!"

"What was it? Some kind of fish, or what?" one officer asked.

"No, I'm telling you, it had claws, like human hands, and you know what I thought of when I looked at the repulsive thing? It looked like a werewolf," Carew said, shaking his head as if to drive away the memory. "It wanted to get me down there and drown me, that's for sure."

"Sir," a police officer asked, "were you swimming in the lake?"

"Of course not," Carew snapped. "I shot a duck, and it fell into the water, and I was trying to retrieve it. Then I heard this mad turmoil beneath me, and that ghastly pointed face was staring at me from the murky depths of the lake."

"One more time, sir, would you describe what attacked you?" the officer said.

"It was furry. I mean, like a wolf, but it was human. It was the ugliest thing I ever saw in my life. I'm telling you, there's something horrendous down there in

Heron Lake. It's sheer madness to be building a tourist resort around that accursed water!" Carew cried in a high-pitched voice.

"Could the thing have been an otter?" the officer asked. "Some of them are pretty large and fierce looking."

"An otter!" Carew cried. "Are you mad? It's not like anything I've ever seen before in my life. It's like something a man who's had too much to drink would see, but I never drink anything stronger than coffee. The whole lake should be condemned!"

Carew spotted Bruce and Jess standing nearby, and he must have recognized Bruce from how his son had described him. "You tell your father to cancel that stupid project. Tell him no tourists are going to want to come to a lake where werewolves are waiting to attack them," he shouted.

Carew refused to go to the hospital to be checked, and he was soon storming off in his pickup truck, muttering, "I never even got my duck!"

"It'll be in all the papers now," Bruce said. "Mr. Carew doesn't want the resort.

He'll make sure it's publicized."

"Maybe that was the whole idea," Jess said.

5 "YOU THINK HE MIGHT have staged it?" Bruce asked.

"I wouldn't put it past him to use all the hysteria about the lake to try to squash the resort project," Jess said. "He's done dishonest things before. You know, a couple of years ago I did a school report on the drownings at Heron Lake. I found out that, except for the one woman, all the other victims were young guys, transients. Nobody like Mr. Carew was ever a victim."

"Like the demon only attacks young transients?" Bruce asked. "What kind of sense does that make?"

"I don't know," Jess said. "Except for Rosemary, that lady, all the dead guys were sort of loners who camped at the lake, made fires, cooked beans, stuff like that. Even Rosemary hung out at the transient camp and bummed cigarettes after her husband left her. That's what the people I talked to told me."

"That's really strange," Bruce said.

"Yeah, and the victims—all but Rosemary—are buried in the poor peoples' plot in the city cemetery where they put dead people who have no survivors. I took pictures of the graves. There are little wooden markers. I found a grave for Arthur Smith, and then there was Willy Anderson. Rosemary is in the main part. Her parents used her maiden name, and they made a nicer marker for her," Jess said.

Jess and Bruce walked back to the car.

The next day, Bruce's parents were really worried. "Look at these newspaper headlines," Bruce's dad groaned. " 'Violent werewolf attacks local man,' 'Is lake in new resort inhabited by monster?' And 'Death lurking in posh new resort lake?' "

"You don't think they'd cancel the whole project over this, do you, Ron?" Bruce's mom asked worriedly.

"I don't know. If this thing gets any bigger, we might just be building a resort that nobody will dare come to, and that is going to dawn on our financial backers. Who wants to frolic in a lake where hideous creatures are trying to drag you down?" Bruce's dad said.

"It's such a shame," Bruce's mom said. "This is the biggest project you've ever done, Ron. With the money you'll earn, we'll have the boys' college educations paid for!"

"I think Mr. Carew staged the whole thing just to spook the investors," Bruce said. "He doesn't want development, and he thinks his stunt will stop it."

"Yes, that's possible," Bruce's dad admitted. "But something is wrong down there. That poor guy who just drowned . . . "

"I bet it was just a simple accident," Layne said. "I bet everybody who drowned just got cramps or something. You know what? I think we should have a big swimming party down at Heron Lake to prove to all these nervous Nellies that there's nothing to be afraid of."

Bruce's dad smiled broadly at Layne. "What a gutsy idea, Layne. I'll be darned if you don't keep surprising me all the time in a really good way," his dad said warmly. "But although I appreciate what you're trying to do, I wouldn't feel right in risking lives. I mean, not that I believe there's some creature down there, but then again, what if there is . . . "

"No way do I want our boys, or any mother's children, swimming in that lake," his mom said firmly. Bruce never saw his mother so set on anything.

"But the idea of a demon down there is stupid," Layne argued.

"I don't care," his mom said. "You don't take chances with the precious lives of children!"

Bruce went to his room, and Layne followed. Before Bruce could close the door, Layne leaned in and said, "I need to talk to you, dude."

"Knock off the dude stuff," Bruce snapped.

"Okay, okay," Layne said softly so their mom and dad wouldn't overhear. "We need to step up to the plate and save Dad's project. It means a lot to him. We need to quietly spread the word that there's going to be a swimming party at Heron Lake. We'll have a funny name for it—like Monster Swim. It's like we're making a joke of the whole scary story, and then people will see us in the water having fun and there goes the horror story."

"Count me out," Bruce said. "I'm not so sure there isn't something evil down there."

"I already talked to Jess, and she's thinking about joining us," Layne said.

Bruce reached out and grabbed a handful of Layne's shirtfront. "You're not getting Jess Grimes in that lake, you hear me? Is that understood? Not her!"

"Shhhh," Layne said. "You want to upset Mom and Dad?" He spoke those words as if he had been in the family from the beginning, like they really were his mom and dad. Bruce resented that. He felt small and cruel to resent it, but he did.

"Okay," Layne continued, "if you're a gutless wonder who won't even help Dad out, then I'll do it myself. I have a few friends. We'll have our swimming party and prove the demon thing is a hoax!"

"Go ahead," Bruce snapped. "Be my guest. If you want to dive into the middle of that cursed lake, go for it!"

Layne usually laughed things like that

off, but now he looked grim. "You hate me, don't you, man? You really hate me," he said.

"I didn't say—" Bruce stammered. But it was too close to the truth to effectively deny it. Bruce never enjoyed his family as much with Layne in it. It was just that he was a stranger, and he spoiled things. Bruce would have welcomed a brother when he was six or seven, but not when he was a teenager. He couldn't adjust to Layne.

"You really do hate me," Layne continued in a harsh voice, "and you know why? Because deep down in your gut you know that I'm a better son to Dad than you are. You sass Dad and argue with him. When Dad tries to rein you in, you give him a hard time."

"I don't do stuff like that," Bruce said.

"Dad works hard, and you don't even tell him how great he is. Are you waiting for him to die so you can say nice things about him at his funeral?" Layne said.

"I feel like busting you in the face for saying a thing like that," Bruce exploded. "You've got no right to talk to me like that.

You aren't my brother. You aren't my parents' son. You're somebody who sneaked into the family like a burglar sneaks into an open window and then takes anything he wants."

"But he likes me better than he likes you, dude," Layne said, "I'm not saying he doesn't love you, but he likes me better. I make him smile and laugh and when he looks at you he's worried about what you're thinking. He's not sure of you. Deal with it. You're second-class, dude. You've got his blood, but I've got his character."

"Shut up!" Bruce hissed.

"Hurts to hear the truth, huh?" Layne said, sneering.

"Shut up or I'll bust your teeth in," Bruce threatened.

"You don't dare. You're a coward. That's why you won't go into Heron Lake to save Dad's project. You're chicken. Chicken!" Layne taunted.

Bruce felt more hatred for Layne than he had ever felt before. "You know what? I hope you go into Heron Lake for your big swimming party, and I hope it gets you! Yeah! So now I've said it. I hope it gets you, whatever it is!" Bruce said.

From the front room their mom called, "You boys aren't fighting, are you?"

"No, Mom," Layne said in his most charming voice.

"Good. It's late. Go to bed," their mom said.

Bruce gave Layne a shove out of his room and then slammed the door in his face. Bruce walked over to the window. He was shaking and perspiring. He had never said anything so awful before in his life.

It was there, in his heart, but he had never said it before. Saying it made it more real, more terrible.

In the morning at breakfast Bruce and Layne avoided even looking at each other. They had never gotten along well, but before they at least could be civil to each other most of the time. But something happened last night. It was like a moment of truth. Bruce didn't think they could ever come back from last night.

Their mom noticed the tension. She kept looking from one boy to the other, searching for clues. Bruce hurried through his eggs and gulped his orange juice. He mumbled something about remembering something he had to tell the sheriff as he fled toward the door. He was going to see the sheriff all right, but not about something he could add to the story. He wanted to find out what Sheriff Dorsett knew about Oliver McGee and the story of the demon in the lake.

The sheriff listened as Bruce told him the story Oliver McGee had related. He chuckled then and said, "Old McGee has been peddling that old chestnut for a good long while, even before I got to be sheriff."

"I was curious," Bruce said, "about the first guy who drowned. They've got him down as John Doe. Did anybody ever figure out who he was?"

The sheriff leaned back in his chair. "Sheriff Weiner was the law back then. He told me the fella was young, a teenager. Maybe 15 or so. The ones who drowned since then were older. Mid-twenties and like that. But he was the youngest. They kept him in the morgue and put out pictures of him dead, thinking somebody would recognize the face. Course, you look different when you're dead . . . " he said.

"But nobody ever claimed him?" Bruce asked.

Sheriff Dorsett sat forward, the palms of his hands on his desk. "Boy, you want to hear something that'll make your hair stand on edge?" he asked.

"Sure," Bruce said.

"Well, one fella came to look at the body. Walt Enright had a missing son and he came . . . " the sheriff said.

"You mean the rich guy on the hill in the big house?" Bruce asked.

"That's the one. He told me his teenaged boy, Todd, had run off and every time he heard about an unidentified body he came to have a look. The man was grieving something fierce. He was maybe 42 or 43, but Sheriff Weiner said he looked 70. Anyway, he took a look at the body, shook his head and walked out without saying a word. Nobody else ever came to have a look at the body, and it was a good thing too," the sheriff said.

"Why?" Bruce asked.

"Because—and this is the scary part—that very night the body disappeared from the morgue. They didn't have real good security in those days. Who'd think somebody would be looking to steal a body anyway? But it was gone. That's how come when you look in the graveyard where the other drowning victims are buried, he's not there. There's no grave for John Doe," the sheriff said.

"Maybe, uh . . . he wasn't really dead," Bruce said.

"Oh no, he was dead all right. He was stiff. Rigor mortis, they call it. He didn't walk out of there under his own steam," the sheriff said.

"You figure the kid was Enright's son?" Bruce asked.

"I don't know. Nobody in town knew the boy. The Enrights came to town about 35 years ago. The wife died shortly after they came. The father sent the boy off to boarding schools. It was a sad story. Enright was fixing to get married again right before the boy disappeared. All that was off when the boy vanished. The fella had money, but not much else. He's been

sitting on that hill alone for 30 years . . . "
the sheriff said, shaking his head.

"Do you still have the picture of the
boy?" Bruce asked.

6 "I GUESS SO. Wait, I'll look in Weiner's files in the back room," Sheriff Dorsett said.

Bruce wasn't sure why he wanted to see the boy's picture. He was thinking that maybe the face he saw under the water that day belonged to the boy. When they showed him photos of the man who drowned, Bruce didn't think it was the man whose face he'd seen. It could have been, but he looked different. But then, like the sheriff said, a photograph of a dead face doesn't look like the real person exactly.

When the sheriff finally emerged, he held a faded old photograph of a gaunt teenager. "He'd been floating in the lake for awhile, so you can't tell much . . . when they fished him out, he'd been banged up on the rocks," Sheriff Dorsett said.

Bruce was entertaining some crazy theory that maybe the boy's ghost remained in the lake, pulling other victims down to share his fate. It was wild, but nothing else was making sense either. But the face in the old picture did not look like the face he saw.

"Look, young fella," Sheriff Dorsett said. "Whoever John Doe was doesn't matter now. Don't be buying into Oliver McGee's madness. Ever since his wife drowned, he's been promoting this demon in the lake theory. If you ask me, she was so upset about what he did that she jumped in the lake. But he doesn't want to face that. It comforts him to think a demon got her. He doesn't want to face it that he's the demon. Those folks who drowned in the lake just drowned, that's all. Nothing pulled them down, if you want my opinion. They all had liquor or drugs in them when they drowned."

"But what about what just happened to Mr. Carew?" Bruce asked.

The sheriff smiled. "You mean the werewolf? I think the guy is trying to put a monkey wrench into the new resort. He wants to set development back a couple of hundred years so he can go on hunting and fishing . . . "

As Bruce walked from the sheriff's office, he glanced up at the Enright mansion on the hill. He wondered what the son—Todd Enright—was like that he would run away from that grand wealthy life and maybe end up in Heron Lake. Maybe, Bruce thought, he felt as angry as Bruce did about something. Sometimes Bruce felt like just disappearing from his family since he got sidelined by Layne. Maybe Todd Enright felt unwelcome too.

On impulse, Bruce decided to drive up the winding private road leading to the Enright estate. He didn't know what he'd do when he got there, but he thought maybe the lonely old man would want to talk about his son.

Bruce didn't really believe that ghosts haunted the spots where they died, yet it was so strange how the body of the first drowning victim had vanished. Maybe it was Todd, and his father had carried him off for a more fitting burial. Maybe he was ashamed to admit what had happened to his son, drinking and dying in Heron Lake. Or maybe the sheriff was wrong. Maybe the boy was not dead. Maybe he got up and walked from that morgue and went to the lake where he now lurks, waiting to push other people under the water. Maybe Todd Enright was the demon.

When Bruce rang the doorbell of the house, he expected a maid or some other servant to answer. Instead, a tall, broad-shouldered man of about 70 stood before Bruce. He was much taller and heavier than Bruce. He was an imposing figure despite his age. "Yes, what do you want?" he demanded in an unfriendly voice.

Bruce had a sinking feeling that it was a big mistake to come here at all. What was he going to do—ask this fierce-looking old man if his son was indeed John Doe, the first to drown in Heron Lake?

"Uh . . . I'm writing a school paper on the history of Heron Springs, and since you've lived here a long time I thought maybe—" Bruce stammered.

The big man said nothing for a few tense seconds. Then the veins in the temples of his bald head bulged in fury. "How dare you?" he growled. "How dare you come to my home and bother me with some idiotic school paper, you stupid punk."

"I—" Bruce gasped, fearing for a moment the old man would strike him. Maybe Layne was right, Bruce thought. Maybe he was a coward. Right now he was covered with goose bumps as he backed away from the man.

"Get off my property! Do you hear me? How dare you disturb my peace! I have guard dogs, and I will call them to tear you from limb to limb if you are not gone in ten seconds. I intend to loose the dogs—rottweilers. They despise intruders as much as I do," the man said.

Bruce hurried back to the car and was barely inside when two vicious-looking dogs came, barking and leaping at the closed windows. Bruce backed up the car, turned around, and sped down the driveway.

"Wow," Bruce groaned to himself when he got back to the main road. He felt sorry for Todd Enright with a father like that. No wonder the kid ran away. Maybe living with the man had driven the boy crazy— crazy enough to lurk around the lake doing terrible things to people.

Or maybe Walt Enright was not the man Bruce had just met back before his son vanished. Maybe the tragedy had twisted and hardened him.

As Bruce was driving down the hill, he noticed a small crowd at the lake. He pulled over on the shoulder of the road and took out his binoculars. He saw Layne and a couple of other guys in swimming trunks. Unlike Bruce, who needed time to build friendships, Layne could pick friends like plucking apples from a tree. Everybody seemed to like him.

As Bruce looked through the binoculars, he saw something then that horrified him. Jess was there in a blue swimsuit! Layne had talked her into being part of the foolhardy scheme. Jess, who swore she would never swim in Heron Lake. Jess, who believed something evil and dangerous was down there. But she was doing it to please Layne. He had sweet-talked her into it!

"The creep!" Bruce screamed as he leaped into his car and raced toward the lake. He had to stop Jess from going in. If

Layne and his stupid friends wanted to risk their lives, it was okay with Bruce. But not Jess.

Bruce was still about a hundred yards from the lake when he saw a dozen people watching. One of them had a video camera. They were clapping their hands and egging on the three boys and Jess, who were wading out into Heron Lake.

"Jess!" Bruce screamed as he stopped and scrambled from the car. He had horrifying visions of watching her disappear, screaming, in the middle of the lake. "Jess, no, come back!"

The crowd on the sand yelled at Bruce. "Knock it off. This is going to be great. We're proving there's nothing bad in the lake so our town gets on the map with the new resort," a boy said.

Jess turned, smiling, and waved at Bruce. "Don't worry, Bruce. It's okay. I was being silly. Anyway, we're all going to be together, so it's perfectly safe. I'm doing this for your dad, Bruce, so he gets to build his resort!" she shouted.

No, Bruce thought, she was doing it for Layne! And he meant to plunge into the water and pull her back before something hideous happened to her. But as he ran for the lake, two boys in the crowd tackled him, throwing him down in the sand.

"You're not going to ruin everything, guy," a big kid yelled. "The girl being in the movie will make it perfect. A cute chick frolicking in Heron Lake. Who could doubt it's safe after that?"

"Let me go," Bruce struggled, but a football-player-sized boy sat straddling him, holding him down. Bruce watched in helpless misery as Jess was going deeper into the lake, right where the demon probably lurked. She was swimming now, laughing. She and Layne were playfully splashing water on each other. Then they swam together, gracefully.

"Hey, don't worry about Jess," a boy laughed. "She's already got a boyfriend, that guy in the water."

The four in the lake were splashing so much that they were surrounded by foamy waves. Bruce couldn't see Jess for a few seconds. Those fools out there were making such a racket that they wouldn't even notice if Jess was dragged under!

"Let me up," Bruce screamed, still struggling, but two guys were holding him down now.

"We're getting great film," the guy with the video camera shouted. "Everybody in town wants the project. It means jobs for our parents. Lots of people are out of work around here. That resort is going to save Heron Springs. After they see this video, nobody is going to be talking about werewolves in the lake anymore!"

The four swimmers were coming in now, still laughing and splashing. They reached the sand and were dancing, making fun of the monster lore. Then, finally, the boys let Bruce to his feet.

Bruce wanted to go to Layne and smash him in the face for what he had done, risking Jess's life. But what good would that do now? Layne was a big hero now. He had dreamed up the whole stunt to save the project, and he had pulled it off without a hitch.

Bruce brushed the sand from his jeans and walked back to his car.

"Bruce," Jess called to him. "You're not mad, are you?"

Bruce didn't turn. He kept on walking. He heard footsteps running after him. Jess seemed really worried about the way he was acting.

"Bruce," she said, reaching him and grasping his arm. "Layne convinced us that we were foolish to believe there was something evil in the lake. He made us laugh our fears away. And we did something good for your dad and the whole town. Bruce, you shouldn't be mad. You should be proud of us."

"He's a big sorehead," Layne said from a few yards off. "He's mad that he was too chicken to go in the water with us. Now that he sees what a big success it was, he's steamed. Don't waste your time, Jess."

Bruce looked right at Jess, into her beautiful dark brown eyes. "What if there is something down there and it got you? How do you think I felt seeing you in the water maybe inches above some clawing fiend? Jess, you told me you believed there was something dreadful down there that grabs people and holds on until they drown. You said that. And then I see you going in the water just because that creep talked you into it. How do you think that made me feel?" he asked.

"Oh, Bruce, I didn't mean to upset you," Jess said in a contrite voice. "But Layne said—"

Bruce interrupted her. "You think I care what he said? It was okay for him to risk his own lousy life, but not yours!"

Bruce looked at Layne standing there with his splendid, athletic body, laughing and toweling off. There wasn't a girl there who wasn't staring at him. He knew how good he looked in his steel-blue swimming trunks, and he was drinking in the admiration. Bruce walked over to Layne and said in a grim voice, "I told you not to get Jess into the water. I told you. I'll get you for this, you creep!" With that Bruce turned and reached his car. He sped off, taking rubber off his tires.

Bruce's face was on fire as he drove, too fast, from the scene. Layne had really done it now. He made a fool of Bruce in front of a bunch of kids who'd be in Heron High with them in just a few weeks. Bruce's reputation would be toast even before he finished his first day. Layne had succeeded in goading Bruce into stupid behavior. As Bruce drove off, he heard kids laughing at him.

Jess wasn't laughing. She was too nice for that. But he could see the respect draining away in her eyes. All she knew was that brave, bold Layne had done this for his dad and nothing bad had happened. The stunt was a smashing success. So why couldn't Bruce join in the celebration?

Jess had seen Bruce in the worst possible light. She would not forget it. It didn't matter anyway. She was Layne's girl now. That was obvious. Just like his dad was Layne's father now. Layne had succeeded in squeezing Bruce out of the picture everywhere.

Bruce got home before his parents or Layne. Layne and his friends, including Jess, were triumphantly taking the video to the TV stations in the neighboring town where Heron Springs got their local news.

Bruce went to his room. He had gone camping many times with his father when he still had a relationship with his dad.

Before Layne. Now Bruce began throwing things in the knapsack and packing in a frenzy.

He didn't belong in this family anymore.

7

BRUCE THREW EVERYTHING he could think of into the bag. It seemed those summer camping trips with his dad were ages ago. It seemed that Layne's shadow had been over his head for a lifetime.

Bruce could imagine how his mom and dad would react to what Layne had done at the lake today. His dad would scold gently, "Now, Layne, I told you it wasn't worth risking lives, but darned if I'm not proud of you, boy. All's well that ends well. Wow, won't those scandal-mongering reporters be mad when they have to admit there's no demon in the lake, that it was just a big hoax?" Bruce's dad would slap Layne on the back. What a wonderful son Layne was. To go all out like that to help his family. His dad would be bursting with pride.

Even his mom, who'd emotionally insisted that "you don't take chances with the precious lives of children," would now forgive Layne for his rashness. She would join in the happy celebration of Layne's ingenuity and courage.

Only one family member would not be there—Bruce. He just couldn't take it. He couldn't stand there and watch Layne take the last drop of his pride away.

Bruce didn't plan to drive into the wilderness. Parking his mom's car at the beginning of a trail would be a dead giveaway to where he was. Instead, he cut through the woods behind the house and jogged at a rapid pace. He left a note behind on the small end table where the mail was stacked for everybody to see.

"Dear Mom, Dad: I need a little vacation from everything. Leave me alone while I sort stuff out. I'll be camping in the wilderness, Dad, just like you and I used to do when we were still a family. Bruce."

As he sprinted along, Bruce felt both exhilarated and brokenhearted. He was getting away from Layne. He wouldn't have to experience another of Layne's victories. Bruce was spoiling Layne's big moment too. That was good. Everybody would be thinking about Bruce taking off, and there wouldn't be much heart for praising Layne. Or maybe not . . .

Maybe everybody would take Bruce's disappearance in stride. Maybe Bruce's worst suspicions were true. Maybe Bruce's place in his dad's heart had been completely taken by Layne. But surely his mom would be upset. Bruce was sorry to be doing this to his mom, but then, she never seemed to notice how much Bruce was hurting. She was saying how wonderful it was how his dad loved Layne. Couldn't she see the pain in Bruce's eyes?

Maybe, in truth, Bruce thought bitterly, nobody, not even his mom, cared that much.

The woods became deep and tangled when Bruce reached the higher elevations. There were little canyons and tiny brooks, even a river. It was the kind of place where you could lose yourself for as long as you wanted, especially if nobody was searching diligently for you. And Bruce figured, at least at first, his parents would give him some time and space. They would wait for him to come home on his own. After all, Bruce was 17. Guys a year older than he was were soldiering halfway across the world. Bruce wasn't a baby anymore. He could take care of himself.

What was that his dad said when he and Bruce last went camping? "You're much better in the wilderness than I am, Bruce. You're a regular pioneer!"

"Yeah, well, belonging to the Boy Scouts hasn't hurt," Bruce had said.

"Of course," his dad had smiled, pride in his eyes. Bruce's dad had swelled with pride every time Bruce won a new badge in Boy Scouts.

Bruce passed a few small caves, then he came to a good-sized cave under an overhanging rock. It was almost completely hidden by trees. He went into the cool little room and sat down on a rock. The Finleys had done a lot of traveling when Bruce was younger. They explored the Carlsbad Caverns in New Mexico, in awe of the Big Room where six football fields would fit. They searched Mammoth Cave and marveled at the miles of passageways. But this was just a modest cave, with enough room to put down a sleeping bag and have a little stretching place.

Still, it looked like a few others had used it over the years. There were rotting candy wrappers and a few beer cans. Bruce glanced around the cave as the rules for exploring caves ran through his memory. Never go into a cave alone was the first rule. Somebody should always know where you are. Well, Bruce had broken the first rule already. But he wasn't a kid. He was almost a man. The final rule was carry three sources of light. Bruce had matches and a flashlight.

Bruce had brought along oat and honey bars to tide him over until he could go fishing. From his cave, using his binoculars, he could see Heron Lake. It was a great place for looking down on the lake.

Bruce was resting in the cave for an hour before his gaze wandered high on the wall to a small crevice. Some object was stuck in the crevice. Bruce pried the object out with his pen knife. It was an old journal, now rotted and missing pages.

Somebody had put it here a long, long time ago. Bruce handled the book carefully. He shone his flashlight beam on the pages that remained, though even they were just fragments.

Bruce finally found a date. The journal had been written 30 years ago. Bruce read snatches of sentences, "He's looking for a new wife. I guess he . . . " Bruce could not read the rest. Then again, "Karen's gonna be the one looks like . . . " Then Bruce read single words on several pages, written in obvious passion, "hate, despise, loathe her, detest, abominate her . . . "

It could be Bruce describing his feelings about Layne! Bruce was stunned. The journal was smoldering with fury. Bruce could feel it rising from the decaying pages as though the feelings were fresh and raw instead of long faded.

Bruce couldn't find any names in the journal except for Karen. But then he found some other items tucked in the back of the journal. A learner's permit. The name was faded out. Apparently the writer of the journal was just learning to drive. Then the report card from

Westchester Military Academy tumbled into Bruce's lap. It was pretty well preserved. The grades were good too, all A's. Bruce gasped when he read the name on the report card, Todd Robert Enright.

Bruce rocked back on his heels. It shocked him to think that 30 years ago a kid like him was running from somebody who had taken his place in his father's heart. Todd was running from his father's girlfriend, Karen. Bruce was running from the brother he never wanted. It was different, yet it was the same.

But where was Todd now, Bruce wondered. Was he still here in some way, an angry ghost visiting Heron Lake from time to time wreaking vengeance on others? Bruce had heard that hatred is one of the worst diseases in the world. It poisons you and turns you into a monster—or maybe a demon. Bruce didn't ever want to hate anybody. Before Layne came along, he never did hate anybody. But now it had overtaken him. He felt helpless against it. It controlled him.

Losing Todd must have destroyed his father's life because he never married

Karen. Mr. Enright still remained a lonely recluse. Bruce figured Todd got his wish. He had ruined his father's life. But at what cost?

But maybe Todd didn't die at all. Maybe that wasn't even him at the morgue. Maybe Todd had left this cave and moved to Switzerland. Or, if it was him, maybe the sheriff was wrong about him being dead. Bruce read about a woman who sat up in a morgue, was taken to the hospital, and survived. Maybe Todd had survived too.

As the darkness of night closed in, Bruce glanced out into the woods. It was spooky, especially when you thought maybe some demon was roaming nearby. It was one thing camping with his father with nothing more serious to worry about than skunks. It was another thing to be looking down on Heron Lake and wondering what lurked beneath its surface.

"Ahhhh," Bruce said aloud, "it's all bunk. There's no demon in the lake. And Todd is not a ghost roaming around. If that was his body in the morgue, his dad got it and buried it in some nice cemetery where there's grass and fountains." Mr. Enright had probably carved beautiful words on the stone about his "beloved son," but while Todd lived he couldn't convince him that he loved him.

Bruce leaned back on his rolled up sleeping bag. He reflected. Wasn't it weird that people waited until their loved ones were dead to tell them on stone and in eulogies how precious they were? Why couldn't Bruce's dad once in a while say, "Bruce, you're my boy, and I love you." He probably thought Bruce already knew. But he didn't. Then again, Bruce had to admit he didn't spend too much time telling his dad that he loved him either.

The normal sounds of the night became sinister to Bruce because of the journal. Even if Todd was long dead, his angry spirit was lurking in the cave like a bad smell.

Bruce noticed something then, down by Heron Lake. There were shadowy figures moving around a campfire. There were maybe two, three men. They were stirring the fire and standing around it.

Bruce looked through his binoculars, and by the light of the fire he could make out the haggard faces of the kind of men who passed through Heron Springs on their way to nowhere. Guys like Willy and Arthur and the last one who died. Transients with drug and alcohol problems. Who people used to call bums. And the spot on this side of Heron Lake became a bum's roost when night fell.

Sometimes, on a warm night like tonight, they took a swim in Heron Lake. And sometimes they did not come out again.

One of the shadowy figures was younger than the other two. He had blonde hair. He looked like he was just a kid. Probably a runaway. Like me, Bruce thought. Like Todd. The other two men looked like veteran transients, though they were probably only in their early twenties. They seemed to be showing the kid the ropes. They were sharing a cigarcttc with him. Probably it was dope.

The kid seemed cold even though it wasn't a chilly night. The men weren't cold, though. They stripped and waded into Heron Lake for a midnight swim.

Bruce stared through his binoculars. There was probably nothing evil in the lake. Look how Layne and his friends frolicked without incident, and yet . . . Bruce trembled as he watched the two transients swimming.

Then the two separated, swimming in different directions. Bruce started shaking. It was like a nervous chill. It was like watching a car bearing down on somebody and being unable to scream.

Suddenly there was just one man in the water, and he was swimming frantically for the shore.

8 "NO," BRUCE GASPED aloud, desperately searching for the other man. It couldn't be happening again. It couldn't be. Some evil crocodile-like creature couldn't be dragging another man to drown at the bottom of the lake!

Bruce watched as the man sprinted across the sand. He and the boy hurriedly packed their meager gear and vanished. There was violent turmoil in one part of the lake, but that had settled down now.

Bruce sank back down to the cave floor. He slept fitfully until dawn. He had planned to catch some fish to fry for breakfast, but he couldn't think of food now. All he could think of was what he'd seen on the lake. Bruce got up slowly. He ached all over. He wasn't used to sleeping in a sleeping bag on the ground.

Then a stick cracked from a footfall. Bruce shrank back into the shadows of the cave, cowering behind the tree branches. A search party? Looking for him? Was it possible? But it sounded like just one man.

Could it be Todd Enright? He would look much different now from the boy who disappeared. He'd probably be gray or bald. He wouldn't look like a monster even though he may be one. Then, suddenly the man came into view.

Oliver McGee!

His gait was uneven. He had been drinking. He stood there staring down at Heron Lake.

"Rosemary," he said in a slightly slurred voice, "the demon that got you got another one last night. Do you know, Rosie? Where you are, do you find out about such things? It wasn't my fault you drowned, girl. I wasn't a good husband to you. I'll own up to that. But I didn't tell you to go down to the lake and smoke with the transients and go swimming in the cursed lake. I never told you to do that. How you died ruined it for me and Doris, you know. I've been a lonely man all these years, girl. But the demon, he's still at it. Got another one last night . . . "

Bruce grabbed his binoculars and looked down at the lake. The law was swarming all over again. Bruce turned numb. It didn't seem possible that it really and truly had happened again. It was up to six now, counting Rosemary. The demon was growing hungrier . . .

In the face of another man's awful death, Bruce felt like a fool for having run away like he did. He was acting like a stupid ten-year-old! A guy was dying down there in the lake, and he was up in a cave hiding from his mom and dad. He was a jerk! But how could he go back now? He would be a laughingstock.

But going back on my own is better than making them hunt for me, Bruce thought. So he packed up his gear and headed down. He'd have to face the music sooner or later, and it might as well be sooner.

Bruce looked through the binoculars one more time. There was a body lying under a yellow tarp. Some people were coming down the hill, a man and a woman. They were running, half stumbling. A young guy followed them.

Bruce felt all the blood rush from his extremities.

It was his mom and dad and Layne! They had heard that the body of a young man had been recovered in the lake, and Bruce was missing. They thought it was him under that yellow tarp!

They reached the body and seemed unwilling to look. Both his dad at one side and Layne at the other side had their arms around his mom. It was so awful Bruce could barely watch the scene below. His mom and dad and Layne clinging together like the survivors of a disaster. But painful as it was, Bruce couldn't take his eyes from it.

"I did this," Bruce groaned to himself. "I put them through this. I'm worse than a crummy son. I'm the absolute pits. No wonder they love Layne better. Who would love somebody like me?"

The sheriff's deputy rolled the tarp from the dead man's face, and suddenly his mom and dad and Layne were all embracing. It was not Bruce. It was some other mother's son.

Bruce was hurrying down the brushy

path now. It had taken him an hour and a half to get here, and it would take almost as long to get down. The minute he saw a pay phone or somebody with a cell phone, he planned to call home.

It would be necessary to pass Heron Lake on the way home, but Bruce didn't think anybody would still be there when he arrived. Of course, the yellow tape that marked a crime scene would still be there, unless the sheriff was still clinging to the belief that all these drownings were accidents.

As Bruce walked, he thought it was odd that Oliver McGee had been roaming around this morning. He knew about the latest drowning too.

Maybe Oliver McGee was the demon in the lake. Maybe he went a little mad when his wife drowned, mostly from guilt. Maybe he wanted to prove the fantasy, over and over, that a demon lurked in the lake and was claiming victims. Maybe it gave him comfort to think that not only Rosemary was pulled down to her death in the lake.

Bruce glanced into his binoculars again.

His parents and Layne were gone. The coroner had arrived, along with several reporters. The monster in the lake theory had new life. Never mind that four brash kids had gone swimming without incident. Two lives had been taken in just the past ten days. Whatever was under the waters of Lake Heron had to be investigated now.

The more Bruce thought about Oliver McGee, the more sense it made that he was behind the drownings. He was clearly relishing the tale of the demon. It was all he talked about. The demon had become his life. Bruce had read about serial killers who wanted their deeds to be known and discussed. That was why so many of them wrote taunting letters to the police and to newspapers.

Bruce walked more cautiously. He didn't want to run into Oliver McGee in the wild. If McGee was the killer lurking under the water and drowning people, he would be dangerous if he thought Bruce had it all figured out.

But it was too late.

"Well, well, fancy running into you in the middle of nowhere," Oliver McGee said, stepping from behind a thicket.

Bruce tried to hide his fear. "Hi. I was just spelunking," he said with a shaky smile.

"What's that?" McGee asked, his eyes narrowing. Was he already suspicious? Did he wonder if Bruce had seen anything from up here last night?

"Exploring caves," Bruce said. "I've been sort of wanting to be a geologist, and so I like to look at formations in the rocks and caves, stuff like that."

"Lot of excitement last night at Heron Lake. Did you see any of it? I know you carry binoculars," McGee asked. Was he fishing?

"I went to sleep early in a cave. I was really tired. Why? What happened?" Bruce asked.

"It got another one," McGee said, his eyes shining with excitement. "Another one in less than two weeks! Can you believe it? I'm telling you, the demon is getting restless. I have a theory, you know. I think it's the first one who drowned that's doing it. Yeah. Way I figure it, that first one who drowned was an accident, but now he's down there in that watery world, and he wants company. So he's bringing some friends down to be with him." Perspiration was popping out of McGee's ugly little face. "See, he got Rosemary first. He must have wanted a girlfriend. Then he gave up on that. He started pulling guys down. You know, Rosie's father liked to have killed me when Rosemary died. He thought I'd pushed Rosie in the lake just so I could go with another girl. But it was a lie. I would never harm the hair on anybody's head. He was blaming me for what the demon did."

"I believe you," Bruce lied.

"You're shaking like an aspen leaf, boy," McGee pointed out.

"I'm just upset that another man died, that's all," Bruce said. "But I believe you, Oliver."

"Do you?" Oliver McGee said in a skeptical voice. "Well, you'll be the first. People just laughed at me when I first told the story. But I guess they're not laughing anymore. Two men in such a short time. I guess that proves there's a demon like I always said."

"I really believe you," Bruce said, getting more nervous by the minute. He wished he was out of the wilderness and back in civilization.

"It grabs 'em and takes 'em down, holds them till they stop shaking," McGee was saying, shaking his head. He looked pale and strange. Maybe it was the whiskey. Then, suddenly, the little man stopped in his tracks and turned to Bruce. "I saw one of them die, you know," he said in a confidential voice.

"You did?" Bruce asked, horrified. Of course he saw one die. He probably saw them all die because he killed them.

"Yep. I'm usually walking around in the woods. I've got nothing else to do. A little hunting, a little fishing. Keeps me going. Anyway, I saw Willie go under. He put up a fight, such a fight. It was the most awful thing I ever did see in my life. Because it wasn't easy to get the best of Willie. I didn't see the demon. It was under the water. But Willie, he kept screaming, 'Let go of me.' He cursed the thing, but it wouldn't let him go. It's so strong. I was scared. I just ran. I knew that even if I went in the water and tried to help Willie, it would have done no good. Then the demon would have gotten me too is all. I knew Willie was a goner so I just ran and saved myself. But I mark Willie's passing. I respect it. Have you seen the oak tree?" Oliver McGee's tone turned solemn.

"Yeah," Bruce said.

"Well then, you see I show them some respect. I write their names on the bark of the oak tree. I call it the drowning tree. It's not right that they're just in that poor cemetery where the unloved and forgotten lie. I put their names on the noble oak. My Rosie and the others. Even the John Does. I'm going to have to carve a new name." A smile came over the man's ugly, little face and he tossed his gray hair with pride. He took out a knife with a glittering blade. "My carving knife," he explained.

Bruce felt ice on his spine.

9 "I . . . UH . . . RESPECT you for doing that, Oliver," Bruce said. "I mean it's a good thing. It would be terrible if they were forgotten."

McGee smiled. "That means a lot to me to hear you say that. Nobody ever told me they respected me before. Not that I deserved it all the time. But you're all right, boy. You're all right. Listen, why don't we walk down by the lake and take a closer look?" he said.

"What?" Bruce asked nervously. McGee wanted to get him near the lake!

"Well, we could talk to the sheriff and find out who the poor guy who drowned was," McGee said.

Bruce looked through his binoculars. The sheriff was still there. Bruce heaved a sigh of relief. But when they got there in about 45 minutes, would Sheriff Dorsett be gone? They seemed to be packing their stuff and just leaving the yellow tape.

"It's a shame," McGee said as they

walked. "It's such a pretty lake. Such a nice lake. Such a dirty shame that this happened. Why did the evil thing have to take up residence in Heron Lake?"

"Yeah," Bruce said. He looked through the binoculars again to see Sheriff Dorsett driving away. "I see the sheriff leaving, so no sense of us getting near the lake. We'll just pass it by quickly."

"Well, let's go to the shore anyway," McGee said. He seemed to be in a very strange mood. "I usually pay my respects to the victim when one of these things happens. Most of the ones who drowned had no special religion, so I do a little ceremony. It's nothing special. I just stand there and remember them and wish them well, like you do when somebody's sailing off on a ship, you know."

"My parents will be meeting me at the lake, I think," Bruce lied, hoping to discourage McGee from planning any violence.

"What were you really doing up there in the wild, Bruce? I don't buy that story that you were looking at caves," McGee asked. He had not called Bruce by his first name before. "Probably you were trying to get away from that adopted brother that you hate so much, huh?"

Bruce was shocked by how on the mark the revolting little man was. "Something like that," Bruce admitted.

"I think hatred has a lot to do with the demon," McGee said in a strangely soft, philosophical voice. "I think if you hate enough, you sort of create demons. I think the demon in the lake is made of hatred."

Bruce looked at McGee and asked, "Do you hate anybody?"

"Plenty of people hate me. The ones that hated me the worst are dead now—Rosie's parents. But I don't hate anybody," McGee said. "The demon down there though. He's from hate. It's like fire and brimstone. You know, Bruce, stop a minute. I'm going to tell you something I've never told anybody, but I like you, so I'm telling you, okay?"

Bruce felt sick and frightened. He didn't want to hear the little man's secrets. Then McGee might think he had to kill Bruce to keep the secrets safe. Bruce was strong enough to overpower McGee if he tried to drag him into the lake, but maybe he had another weapon besides the knife, like a gun.

"You don't have to tell me anything that's a secret," Bruce said.

"No, no. I want to tell you. I know I said to you before that I've never seen the demon, but that wasn't true. I did see him one dark night. I know you won't laugh when I tell you, because you said you respect me. But I swear I saw the demon the night Willie died. I saw it for just an instant rising out of the water, like some seaweed-covered monster. Right after it got Willie . . . " McGee said.

"Did you tell the sheriff?" Bruce asked.

"You think he would have believed me? He mocks me," McGee said. "The old sheriff before him thought for a long time that I killed Rosie."

They were nearing the lake now. Bruce could see the pay phone. His heart began to pound. He needed to call, and quick.

"Bruce," McGee cried, grabbing Bruce's wrist. "There's something in the water right now."

Bruce looked but he couldn't see anything.

"The water is stirring!" McGee said shrilly. "Don't get any closer or the demon is going to see us. It's down there waiting for prey!"

Bruce believed McGee was out of his mind now. He feared more than ever that he was the one drowning people. The spells probably overtook him, and he went mad. "I've got to call my parents," Bruce said.

"You can't," McGee said in an agitated voice. "Oh, look at how the water is roiling now. I think it's coming out. If it sees us, boy, it'll drag us right into the water like the crocodiles do!" McGee turned pale then and he screamed, "It's coming out! Run! Boy, run for your life!"

Bruce didn't move, but McGee took off like a rabbit, vanishing behind the trees that rimmed the lake. Bruce hurried toward the pay phone, but before he reached it, he saw what had terrified McGee—rising from the water.

Bruce almost turned and ran too, but then he saw it was only a man in a diving suit. Probably someone from the sheriff's department investigating what was going on here. The diver emerged from the water and clambered onto the beach. He was still wearing his facemask as he kicked off his flippers on the sand. He seemed to be staring at Bruce through the facemask.

"Hi," Bruce called to him. "You must be with the sheriff, huh?"

The man spit out his snorkel that he breathed with. He said in a gruff voice, "You're the one that bothered me at my home, aren't you?"

"Mr. Enright?" Bruce gasped in surprise. He didn't expect a man in his seventies to be helping with the police investigation even if he was a diver. He was probably volunteering to help. A tiny town like Heron Springs didn't have much money to pay professionals.

"What are you doing here?" Enright demanded. "Waiting for dusk, eh? You're one of the transients, aren't you?"

"No, no," Bruce said.

"Probably stole that car you were driving the other day. Lot of you transients are dirty thieves," Enright said.

"It was my mom's car. She let me borrow it," Bruce said. "I'm going to call my parents right now to come pick me up."

"You're a runaway, aren't you?" Enright demanded, coming closer.

"No, I just went off into the hills to camp for a day," Bruce said.

"I know a runaway when I see one," Enright said. He was a tall man, and he seemed to tower over Bruce.

"Excuse me, sir," Bruce said. "I need to go over to that pay phone and call my parents."

"You haven't seen your parents in years. I know the look of you. Believe me, I have reason to know very well. My son ran away when he was 15. My son, Todd. Just 15. He was doing so well in school. He ran away into the hills. I never found him again until they called me down to the morgue to look at a body they had fished from this lake." Mr. Enright's voice came in hot, angry spurts, like lava spouting from a volcano.

Bruce wasn't surprised. He had thought the first drowning victim, John Doe, was

Todd Enright. Now he shuddered at the thought of what this man had gone through. Bruce remembered the appearance of his own parents staggering across the sand in terror to look at the face beneath the yellow tarp. "I'm sorry, Mr. Enright," he said. "I'm sorry about your son."

"My boy wasn't a dirty transient like the rest of you," Enright said in a savage voice. "He wasn't a dirty dope-sniffing transient hanging at the camp. He was a good boy, a good family boy. He was the best son a man ever had. But they lured him away from home, those dirty transients, camping down here by the lake. They taught him to use drugs and to turn against his blood."

Bruce figured Mr. Enright never got to read the bitter journal Todd had written and left in a crevice in the cave. Then he might have understood. Then again, a man like Enright probably never would have understood anything he didn't want to believe. He wouldn't believe the truth if it hit him in the face.

"I don't use drugs. I never have. I live

right down the road with my family,"
Bruce said.

"The devil take your lies because I'm
not believing them," Enright snarled.
"Guys like you lured my son away. They
taught him to smoke dope and get drunk.
They urged him to go swim in Heron Lake
when he was drunk and drugged, and they
laughed when he went down and never
came up again. I didn't see it happen, but I
know that's how it was. I didn't ever get to
see my son alive again. They were going
to bury him in that plot where people
nobody cares about are buried. My son,
the person I loved more than anybody else
on earth."

Bruce stared at the man, horror coming
to life inside him. He desperately wanted
to make a dash for the phone booth about
ten yards away. But he feared any sudden
moves might trigger violence in the man.

"I carried his body off in the night from
their morgue. I took my Todd to a
beautiful memorial park and put him
under a marble stone fit for a young
prince because that's what he was,"
Enright's voice began to shake violently

with emotion. "He was my life, my future. All the money I made was for my son . . . for his future, but they took his future away. They took everything . . . "

"I'm really sorry about what happened to your son," Bruce said. His heart rate was rising. Something was wrong here. Something was terribly wrong. Bruce glanced at the phone booth. He had to somehow get there. If he did, he wouldn't waste time calling his parents. Now he would call 911.

Bruce was young and quick, and this man was 70 years old. Surely Bruce could beat him to the phone booth and get in those three numbers—911. He had to try. Bruce wheeled and took off toward the pay phone, but he didn't get more than two yards before Enright grabbed his arm and held it like a vice. "You don't want to call your parents," he snarled. "You want to call your dirty friends and tell them it's time to meet and make a fire and smoke dope like you do every night."

"Please, Mr. Enright, you're all wrong about me," Bruce said. "Will you let me call my parents? You can talk to them too, and then you'll see I'm telling you the truth."

"You need to go for a swim, you dirty transient," Enright said. "Look at you. Dirty shirt, dirty jeans. You're all dirty and evil. Yes, you need a swim in Heron Lake." Enright started dragging Bruce toward the lake. Real terror set in now. Bruce tried desperately to dig the heels of his sneakers into the dirt and stop the forward progress, but Enright was incredibly strong. Bruce only weighed 160 and this man topped 200, mostly muscle.

"Stop hanging back," Enright screamed, turning and slapping Bruce across the face in a stinging blow. Bruce tasted blood in his mouth as he went sprawling across the sand. Then the old man stood over him and screamed, "You killed my son. You killed Todd, my boy, my only son. You and your kind did it. You are all the same. You are scum on the water. You are a pestilence on the earth that must be stamped out. You lured my boy from his home where he was happy and loved, and you let him drown like a rat in the cold water."

Bruce looked up at the madman who towered over him.

"You're all wrong! When I was in the hills I came to a cave where Todd stayed. He left a journal there. He thought you didn't care about him. He was hurt that you were going to marry some lady named Karen. He hated her. He ran away because he hated Karen," Bruce shouted, hoping the information might shock the man back to sanity.

Enright kicked Bruce savagely in the ribs. "Liar! My boy loved Karen as much as I did. What journal? He never kept a journal. He was happy for me that I found another woman to love. She was to be his mother. He was so happy to have a new mother. How dare you tell such lies!" Enright screamed.

Bruce recalled the many words for hate that Todd had scrawled bitterly in the journal. But reminding the man of the real reason his son ran away only made him angrier.

"Let me go," Bruce pleaded, "I didn't do anything to you. I wasn't even born when your son died! Let me go!"

Walter Enright reached down and grabbed Bruce's arms, dragging him to his feet. Then he caught him from behind in an iron bear hug. "We will walk to the water and you will go in," Enright said. "You will go into Heron Lake where my son died . . . "

10 AS ENRIGHT PUSHED Bruce forward, Bruce fought every inch of the way. He kicked back at the man behind him, trying to cause such pain in his shins that he would release his hold. But the kicks seemed to have no effect. The old man seemed to be made of steel. He was like a terrible machine, holding Bruce in his grip, holding Bruce's arms against his body and gripping his chest so tightly that Bruce was having trouble breathing.

Every second brought them closer to the edge of Heron Lake. They moved as one, relentlessly forward.

"The woman was as bad as the men," Enright said. "She hung down at the camp and smoked with them. She was a transient too. I don't regret what happened to her. She was one of the ones who lured my son to his death. They all had a part in it," Enright raved. "Last night, two of the transients had a blonde

boy with them. He looked just like Todd.
Todd was a blonde, a handsome blonde
boy . . . they were luring the blonde boy
into smoking dope, just like they lured my
Todd. You were there with them."

"I wasn't," Bruce gasped. He was
getting dizzy. He thought he'd pass out at
any moment. Then all Enright had to do
was pitch him into the lake, and he would
drown.

"I took one of the transients down to
where you all belong . . . to the bottom of
the lake with the water lice and the beetle
larvae and the horse leeches. That's where
you will be in a few minutes . . . " Enright
said.

From the corner of his eye, Bruce saw
something move out of the thicket of
trees. Bruce caught a glimpse of Oliver
McGee, a knife in his hand. Bruce used
every ounce of strength he had to wrench
away from the old man holding him, while
at the same time he kicked back, inflicting
pain. For just a second, Enright loosened
his hold on Bruce, but he still could not
escape his grasp. But McGee used that
second of distraction to leap behind

Enright and plunge the knife between his shoulder blades.

Walter Enright let out a great howl and dropped to his knees. He was not mortally wounded, though, and there was every indication he would recover and become a threat again.

"I've got some rope," McGee yelled. "Help me tie him up while he's in shock." Working feverishly, they bound the man's hands and feet as he floundered on the sand. "Those are good knots," McGee said. "I was a sailor once."

"You saved my life," Bruce said.

Oliver McGee grinned. "Well, you were the only one who ever said you respected me," he said.

"It's the demon, isn't it?" Bruce said, looking at Enright.

"Yep, it's him all right," McGee said.

"You were right," Bruce said. "He's made of hate just like you said."

"Yep," McGee said before calling 911.

The sheriff and Bruce's parents arrived minutes later. His mom and dad ran down the hill, followed by Layne. Bruce's dad got there first, throwing his arms around

Bruce. "Son, we were sick with worry. When we heard a young man drowned, we almost died of fright."

"I'm so sorry," Bruce said. "I'm sorrier than I can put into words."

Bruce's mom hugged Bruce then. She was crying. Bruce kept saying, over and over, "I'm so sorry, you guys."

Layne stood a little aside, taking awkward glances at the reunion scene. Bruce felt something strange—it was like a fever breaking and the poison draining away from a person's body. It was the hatred draining, leaving Bruce suddenly free. "Hey, dude," Bruce said, "haven't you got a welcome hug for your brother?"

A grin splashed across Layne's face. He leaped into Bruce's opening arms, and they danced on the sand like two football players who'd just won the Super Bowl.